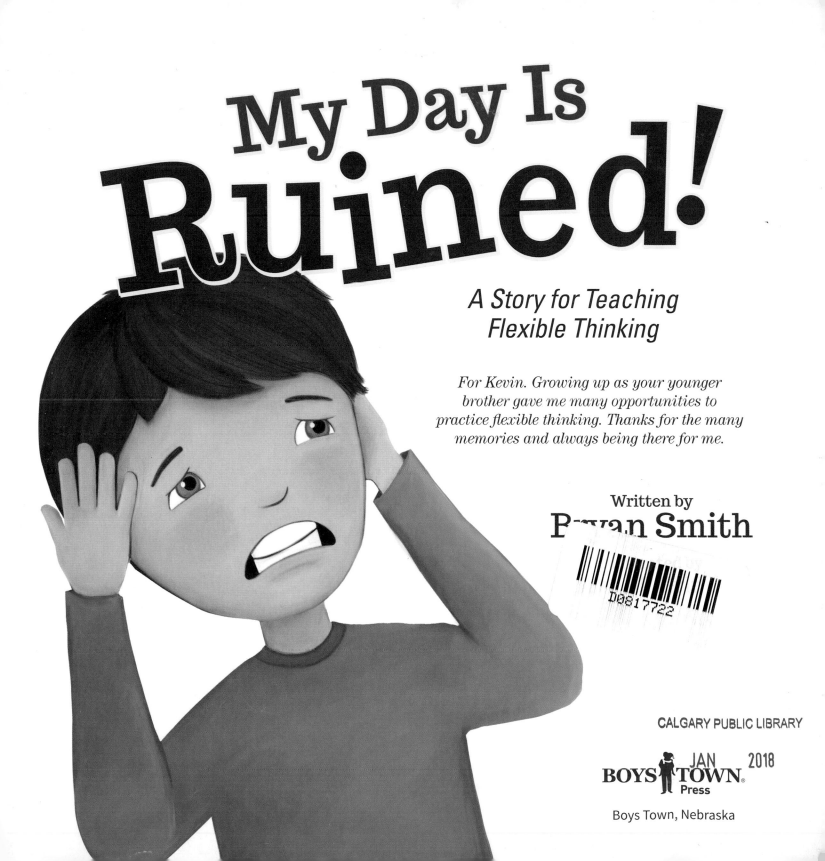

My Day Is Ruined!

A Story for Teaching Flexible Thinking

For Kevin. Growing up as your younger brother gave me many opportunities to practice flexible thinking. Thanks for the many memories and always being there for me.

Written by
Bryan Smith

BOYS TOWN
Press

Boys Town, Nebraska

My Day Is Ruined!
Text and Illustrations Copyright © 2016 by Father Flanagan's Boys' Home
ISBN: 978-1-944882-04-4

Published by the Boys Town Press
14100 Crawford St.
Boys Town, NE 68010

For a Boys Town Press catalog, call **1-800-282-6657**
or visit our website: **BoysTownPress.org**

Publisher's Cataloging-in-Publication Data

Names: Smith, Bryan (Bryan Kyle), 1978- author. | Griffin, Lisa M. (Lisa Middleton), 1972- illustrator.

Title: My day is ruined! : a story for teaching flexible thinking / written by Bryan Smith ; illustrated by Lisa M. Griffin.

Description: Boys Town, NE : Boys Town Press, [2016] | Audience: grades K-6. | Summary: When the championship baseball game gets rained out, ballplayer Braden curls up on the couch and cries. Just another one of his overreactions. Braden always lets small disappointments ruin his day, so his mom and teacher give him a lesson on "flexible thinking." Will this help Braden feel better when disappointment comes his way?--Publisher.

Identifiers: ISBN: 978-1-944882-04-4

Subjects: LCSH: Disappointment in children--Juvenile fiction. | Emotions in children--Juvenile fiction. | Adaptability (Psychology) in children--Juvenile fiction. | Personality in children--Juvenile fiction. | Children--Life skills guides. | CYAC: Disappointment--Fiction. | Emotions--Fiction. | Change--Fiction. | Personality--Fiction. | Conduct of life. | BISAC: JUVENILE FICTION / Social Themes / Emotions & Feelings.

Classification: LCC: PZ7.S643366 M9 2016 | DDC: [Fic]-dc23

Printed in the United States
10 9 8 7 6 5 4 3

Boys Town Press is the publishing division of Boys Town, a national organization serving children and families.

Hey everyone.
My name is Braden and I'm in the third grade.

How many of you out there just hate it when someone **ruins your day** and then acts like YOU'RE the one who's wrong?

It happened to me again, just the other day.

4

My teacher, Mrs. Vickerman, acted like it was my problem for getting upset because the principal ruined my day AGAIN by having a fire drill in the middle of free reading time. (And I was ALMOST finished with my book!) She said she was going to call my mom and discuss some ways to help me use more *"flexible thinking."*

Mrs. Vickerman kept going on and on about flexible thinking this and flexible thinking that, but all I heard was

"BLAH BLAH BLAH."

The good news is that two whole days went by and I didn't hear anything about flexible thinking from my teacher or my mom. **Cha ching!** They finally must have decided to **LEAVE ME ALONE!** Now I could focus on the championship baseball game I'm playing in tomorrow.

I had waited all eight years of my life for this day! And I just knew we were going to win because we had already beaten the team we were going to play earlier in the season! So when I woke up the morning of game day, I looked around my room to figure out where I was going to put my championship trophy. Then I quickly threw on my uniform and went downstairs to eat breakfast.

As I walked around the corner to the kitchen, I immediately froze.

NOOoooooooooo!

I could feel tears welling in my eyes as I saw the rain pouring down outside. **"Why do things like this always happen to me?**

My day is ruined!"

I plopped down on the couch and covered myself with a blanket.

"I know," Mom said. "This really stinks. You were so excited. But sometimes we have to roll with the punches. Truthfully, the rain is something we can't control, but what we can control is what we're going to do now that it is raining."

"Mom, you just don't understand," I said.

"You weren't the one who was going to get a

humongous trophy

and become famous. I was going to be on the morning announcements at school on Monday."

"You're right," Mom replied. "I don't know exactly how you feel, but it still stinks for me, too. I was really excited to get to watch you play ball."

LOCAL TEAM WINS THE CHA

t
in
bas
ama
the
team
At the
struck
homeru
the park
as the cr
following
batters in.
Record sea
star player.
in spectacula
the play ende
baseb 9 .ns.
the team had a
He was voted
Ex

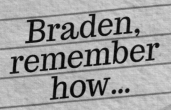

"Oh great, here we go again," I thought.

"Don't you guys know you can't really stretch your brain?" I said.

"It doesn't exactly mean that," Mom said. "It basically means you need to get creative with your thinking. When one thing doesn't work, don't give up. Try something else instead... like this!"

brain stretching = flexible thinking

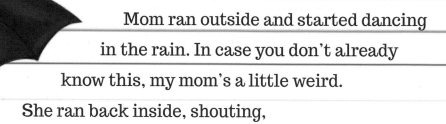

Mom ran outside and started dancing in the rain. In case you don't already know this, my mom's a little weird. She ran back inside, shouting,

"I've got it!

This rain isn't going to stop us!

We're still going to have a baseball game today!"

A few minutes later, she had laid out a slip-and-slide and some bases in the back yard.

Before long, a bunch of my friends showed up and we had our first **rainy day slip-and-slide** baseball game. Don't tell my mom, but I think I had more fun playing this than playing our real game.

13

That night, as Mom put me to bed,
she whispered, "Did you see how I used flexible thinking today?"

"Yeah. I wish I could think like that."

"You can. Just follow these four steps."

#1 **Take a deep breath.**

#2 **Realize some things are out of your control.**

#3 **Change your plan.**

#4 **Accept the change.**

"Yeah," I said. "I guess I didn't do any of those things today, but next time I will!"

Later that week, we were in math class learning how to solve different equations. The first one was easy: 6+5= ? I quickly wrote down 11.

Mrs. Vickerman said,
"Great. Tell me how you know that's right. You need to prove it."

"Uh, you can ask my mom?"
I said. "I'm not sure how else to prove it."

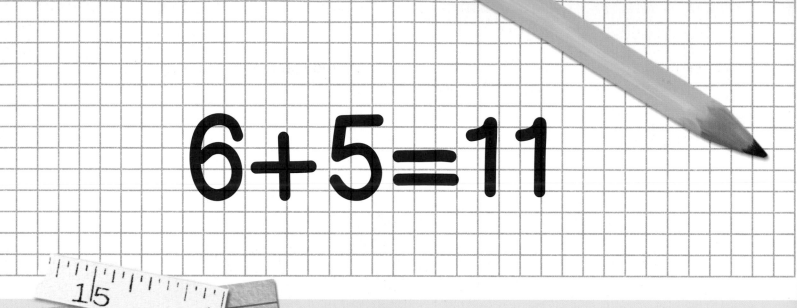

6+5=11

FLEXIBLE THINKING

Mrs. Vickerman told me I could draw an example, use my hundreds chart, or use a number line. Now I kind of remember her teaching us those, but to be honest, I wasn't listening because I don't see why you have to solve problems in more than one way. Since I didn't agree with her, I just wrote it bigger: **6+5=11.**

"Braden, all you did was make it bigger," she said. "That's not really showing me a different way. You have to use *flexible thinking.* Your mom told me she shared our plan with you. Let's try it here."

"How about step **#1,** Take a deep breath? Did you remember to do that?"

STEP #1

"No."

"Well give it a try now."

"Fine."

I took a deep breath.
That part wasn't hard.

17

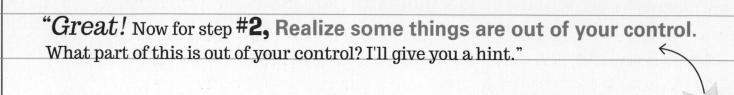

"*Great!* Now for step **#2, Realize some things are out of your control.** What part of this is out of your control? I'll give you a hint."

STEP #2

"Who decides how many ways you have to show your answer?"

"Uh, you."

"*Right.* So you don't have any control over that."

STEP #3

"Let's go to step **#3, Change your plan.** You were trying to do something the same way and didn't even try the other examples I offered. Now that you're ready, let's try it again." Then she reminded me of the other ways. I decided to try and draw it out.

"Wait, can I draw baseballs?" I said.

"Sure," she said.

I quickly drew a picture with six baseballs and then drew five more. Below them I wrote the number 11.

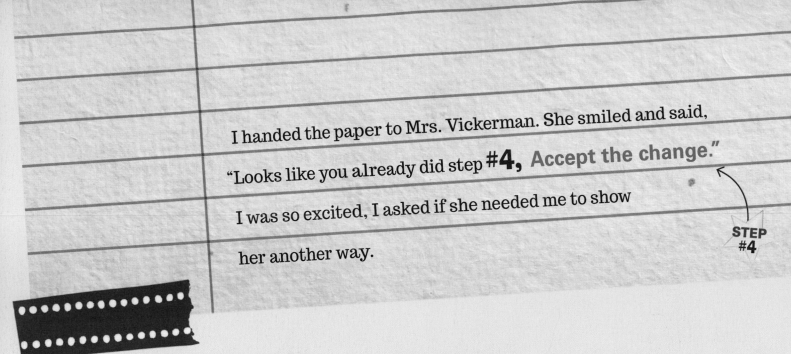

I handed the paper to Mrs. Vickerman. She smiled and said, "Looks like you already did step **#4, Accept the change."**

STEP #4

I was so excited, I asked if she needed me to show her another way.

"I don't think so. You already showed me you know how to solve it in more than one way. *But more importantly, you showed me you know how to use flexible thinking."*

The next day at lunch, I was looking forward to eating our cafeteria's famous jumbo corn dogs. I hated being last in line, but the wait was certainly going to be worth it. As I waited, I could smell the...

Whaaat??! That smells like tomato soup.

Sick. I hate that. I put my tray back and started to march right over to the cafeteria worker to tell her how **my day was ruined!**

Yuck!

21

That's when it clicked. I remembered the plan Mom and Mrs. Vickerman showed me. **I took a deep breath.** That's when I overheard the cafeteria worker telling another student the corn dogs were left out and went bad, so they had to think of something else to serve for lunch.

Huh! That sounds just like flexible thinking.

If they can do it, so can I.

I looked around... I saw there was celery with peanut butter. There were also crackers for the soup. There had to be a way I could make this work. Duh! I could just make peanut butter crackers for lunch and wash them down with some chocolate milk.

As I sat down to eat, my teacher came over and gave me a high-five. "Looks like someone is using his **flexible thinking**."

I smiled. It wasn't my favorite lunch, but I sure felt great leaving the lunchroom!

FRIDAY:
SCHOOL SPIRIT
ASSEMBLY

On Friday, we were going to have a fun school assembly where everyone wore their school spirit shirts. That morning, my brother Blake came down and saw me in my spirit shirt. "Oh yeah! I forgot," Blake said.

He sprinted back to his room to change.

That's when
things went

downhill.

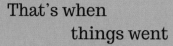

He looked everywhere
and couldn't find his shirt.
"Mom, where's my school spirit shirt?"
Blake asked. "It's dirty," Mom said.
He didn't care. He went through the
dirty clothes, found it, and threw it on.

"Nasty!"

I said.

Mom came out and told him he could not wear the dirty shirt to school. So Blake turned it inside-out, figuring Mom wouldn't realize it was the same shirt.

"Nice try, bud," Mom said, "but it needs to come off. Let's try some flexible thinking."

"No fair!" Blake said. **"My day is ruined!"** I guess no one had ever really shown him how to use flexible thinking.

NO FAIR! My day is ruined!

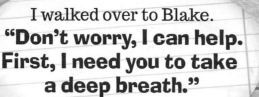

I walked over to Blake. **"Don't worry, I can help. First, I need you to take a deep breath."** He did.

"Great. Sometimes some things are out of your control. I know you really want to wear your shirt, but that's not an option. Mom's not going to let you. You need to change your plan. Let me help you. What are our school colors?"

"Black and red," he said.

"Right. Why don't we just find a shirt that has the school colors on it?"

"Hmmm... okay," he said.

He went to his room and found a superhero shirt he wanted to wear. **"Uh Blake, I'm not sure if your light was on in your room, but that shirt's NOT black and red!"** I said.

Blake just looked at me and smiled.

Overreacting is common for children,

but as they get older, it becomes more important that they learn to manage their emotions and practice flexible thinking. Start early by using the tips below:

1. **Try and set children up for success.** If a child is very excited about doing something fun or a specific event, set expectations with the child. Remind him or her of all the fun activities that might be involved, and role-play what other options might be available if the one he or she is most excited about is not an option.

2. **Spend some time helping children practice** how to adjust to changes they may or may not be expecting. For example, take an ordinary board game and make up new rules. Explain the rules and try to have fun! This will help the child adjust to new rules and let his or her imagination run wild!

3. **Encourage children to get out of their comfort zones** and try something new. This will help them avoid getting fixated on routines.

4. **Be a role model for children.** Think out loud and then act so the child can see how you use flexible thinking to help solve problems.

5. **At dinner or in a small group at school,** have each family member or class member say what the best and worst part of his or her day was and what he or she did (or could have done) to make it better.

6. **Find examples of flexible thinking** in favorite stories or TV shows, and use that time to talk to children about what they're seeing.

7. **Look for role models** in the real world who faced challenges and overcame them, and talk to children about what they did (e.g., athletes who have been successful despite missing limbs; musicians who are very talented and work beyond challenges like not being able to see).

Most importantly, remember that children are always watching and learning. The way you react to challenging situations is the best lesson you can teach a child.

So BE what you want to SEE!

For more parenting information, visit boystown.org/parenting.

BOYS TOWN ®
Parenting

Boys Town Press Featured Titles
Kid-friendly books to teach social skills

Executive **FUNction**

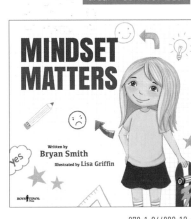

WITHOUT LiMiTS
dream•connect•soar

What Were You **Thinking?**
Written by **Bryan Smith**
Illustrated by Lisa M. Griffin

978-1-934490-85-3

Downloadable Activities
Go to BoysTownPress.org to download.

My Day Is **Ruined!**
A Story for Teaching Flexible Thinking
Written by **Bryan Smith**
Illustrated by Lisa. M. Griffin

978-1-944882-04-4

Of COURSE It's a **Big Deal!**
A Story about Learning to React Calmly and Appropriately
Written by **Bryan Smith**
Illustrated by Lisa. M. Griffin

978-1-944882-11-2

MINDSET MATTERS
Written by **Bryan Smith**
Illustrated by Lisa Griffin

978-1-944882-12-9

Is There an **App for That?**
Written by **Bryan Smith**
Illustrated by **Katie Wish**
Hailey Discovers HAPPiness through Self-Acceptance

...There an **pp for That?**
Activity Guide
Written by **Bryan Smith**
Illustrated by **Katie Wish**
...ons to Teach and Reinforce ...eptance and Positive Changes

978-1-934490-74-7   978-1-934490-75-4

IF WINNING ISN'T **EVERYTHING, WHY DO I HATE TO LOSE?**
Written by **BRYAN SMITH**
Illustrated by **BRIAN MARTIN**

The National Parenting Center *Seal of Approval*

978-1-934490-85-3

IF WINNING ISN'T **EVERYTHING, WHY DO I HATE TO LOSE?**
...each and Reinforce Displaying Good ...p at School, in Athletics and at Home

978-1-934490-91-4

Kindness Counts
a story for teaching random acts of kindness
Written by **Bryan Smith**
Illustrated by **Brian Martin**

978-1-944882-01-3

Downloadable Activities
Go to BoysTownPress.org to download.

BOYS TOWN® Press

For information on Boys Town, its Education Model, Common Sense Parenting®, and training programs:
boystowntraining.org | boystown.org/parenting
training@BoysTown.org | 1-800-545-5771

For parenting and educational books and other resources:
BoysTownPress.org
btpress@BoysTown.org | 1-800-282-6657